British Library Cataloguing in Publication Data

Hackney, Jo
  Alec's dragon.
  I. Title   II. Series
  823'.914 [J]

  ISBN 0-340-51427-2

First published 1990

Published by Hodder and Stoughton Children's Books,
a division of Hodder and Stoughton Ltd,
Mill Road, Dunton Green, Sevenoaks, Kent TN13 2YA

Photoset by Litho Link Ltd, Welshpool, Powys, Wales

Printed in Great Britain by St Edmundsbury Press Ltd,
Bury St Edmunds, Suffolk

Contents

Damian the Dragon
Chapter 1

A lec was cleaning his teeth. This was the last part of his Saturday morning routine in the bathroom. Sometimes he spent hours in there. His mum worked on Saturdays so that meant Alec could spend as long as he liked, doing *what* he liked. As long as he tidied up afterwards.

Anyway, this particular Saturday Alec had stayed in bed even longer than usual. He'd been reading about a boy called Eustace Scrubb who turned into a dragon because ... but that's another story. Alec had also been eating a stick of rock in bed. I suppose that's why he was paying so much attention to his teeth.

'Where have I put my glasses?' he muttered to himself. 'I need another pair so I can find the ones I've just taken off.' He groped around. 'Ah, here they are. Now what's that funny noise?'

Alec talked to himself rather a lot. He liked his own company, his books, and the fantastic games he made up along the lines of *Dungeons and Dragons*. His mother said he was just a loner. She sometimes worried, though, because he didn't seem to have any friends.

'Hope it's not a mouse,' he said round his toothbrush. He put his glasses on and peered round the bathroom. Then he noticed something very, very odd in the lavatory. 'Hell's bells!' he said. 'It's a baby dragon!'

He stood and stared at the little reptile for ages. It gazed back at him and seemed just as surprised. Finally he said, 'What are you *doing* down there? Ugh, you must be all covered in something horrible.'

He wrinkled his nose as he lifted the thing from the lavatory bowl. 'Pooh, you *stinker*! You're going straight in the bath.'

While he ran the water Alec studied the

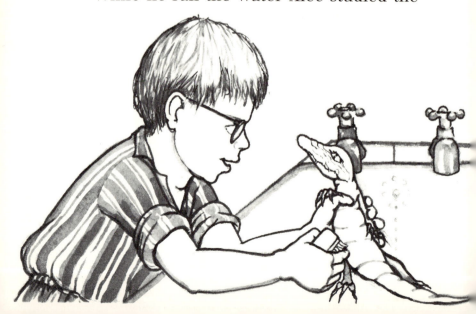

baby dragon, turning it over in his hands.
It felt smooth and wet, but not slimy.
It *was* very smelly, though. After he'd
tested the water with his elbow Alec put
the thing in the bath and started to scrub
it with the nailbrush. Strangely enough it
didn't struggle or wriggle about. It seemed
to enjoy having its tummy done.

'You little monster,' Alec said fondly.
'Fancy coming out of the loo like that –
Hey, I'm glad I wasn't sitting on it!'

He studied its scaly back. He thought he
could see where its wings were just
starting to grow. 'Wait till you see my
dragon games and things,' he said as he
cradled it in a towel on his knees. 'Course
you'll have to stay in my room when
Mum's here. I dunno whether she'll like
me having my own dragon. Still, she *did*
offer to get me a puppy as long as I
cleaned up after it. Oh no, look at the
mess in *here*! I bet it's dead late too. She'll
be home soon.' He went out into the

hallway of the flat to look for something to put his dragon into while he cleaned the bathroom.

He spotted the washing-basket on the floor and dumped his pet into it, towel and all. 'Just stay there a bit – she'll go *spare* if she sees this. Where's all this water come from?' He mopped up the wet floor with the soggy bath-mat and used half a bottle of Jif to clean the bath. Then he wished he hadn't because it took ages to rinse it all off.

He dashed off into the kitchen to put the bath-mat and his wet pyjamas into the washer, under some sheets that were already in there. Then, of course, the doorbell rang. Groaning, he grabbed one of the sheets and wrapped it round himself. He raced into the hall, scooped up the wash-basket and its curious contents and dumped it in his room. He closed his door on the edge of the sheet but managed to stretch it enough to cover his modesty while he opened the front door.

'Whatever have you been doing, Alec?' Mrs Biggs from the flat opposite stood

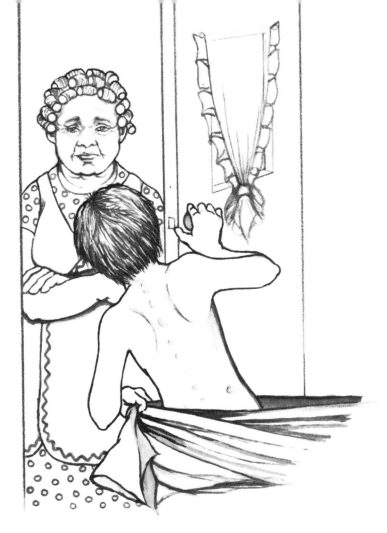

there in pinafore and curlers. 'Racing
round like a mad thing – aren't you
dressed yet? Lazy lump. Give me your
mum's washing, I might as well peg it out
with mine. Be dry in half an hour,
I reckon. *You* should be outside, lovely day
like this. Can't remember a better July.
Come on then, love, chop-chop.'

Alec clapped his hand to his head.
'No! Er, sorry Mrs B. – only I promised I'd
do it. I'll just get dressed then.' He started
to close the door, grinning stupidly at her.

'Humph – can't imagine *you* doing that –
you won't do it right, anyway.'

'Oh I will, honest. It's OK, Mrs B. I – um –
I *want* to, see. I want to do a bit more to
help Mum, with her working and
everything.'

'Aaah, bless him. What a nice thought,
Alec.'

Alec thought she was going to hug him
and stepped back hastily. He closed the
door, and with a ragged sound the sheet
ripped and freed him. 'Oh hell, what'll I do

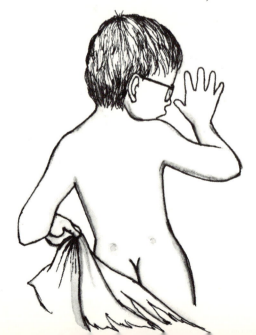

now?' He sat on the floor and his bare bottom made a plopping sound on the lino.

Alec decided to wash the sheet in two halves and explain later. It was a good job he looked in on his dragon first, because it had had an accident on some of *that* washing so he had to do that, too. At least the dragon could sleep in the wash-basket now. Alec put a few of his tee-shirts in the bottom to make it more comfy. By the time he'd finished his mum was due home so he squashed the basket under his bed. He thought he'd better find out what baby dragons like to eat. . .

When his mum looked in after tea, everything seemed normal – Alec sitting with his nose in a book. She was a bit surprised that he had fetched the washing in and folded the sheets and put them away without being asked. He can't be sickening for something, she thought. After all, he ate all of his tea in record time, then asked for second helpings.

Since it was such a beautiful evening, Alec's mum said she'd walk along by the river and look in on Grandad's allotment before she went to visit him. Grandad hadn't been well lately and he couldn't get there. Mum had been on at Alec to go and do some weeding, but, so far he'd managed to find excuses not to. His mum said he was allergic to fresh air and exercise. She didn't insist, though.

The truth is, she really spoiled Alec. It was easier to give in to him, and he was a good boy really. Grandad would say, 'That boy needs a father's firm hand,' and then proceed to spoil him just as much.

You can imagine how surprised his mum was when Alec offered to go with her. 'I'll get Grandad's shed keys off him,' he said. 'Then I can use his gardening gloves and things – I don't want to go picking up creepy-crawlies with my bare hands, do I?'

'Well, you could have borrowed my rubber gloves any time,' Alec's mum said. She laughed and patted his cheek. 'Just make sure you keep that shed locked. You know Grandad thinks those hippies will start squatting in there if they get the chance.'

When they got back from Grandad's, Alec went straight to his room to read before bed, as usual. He pulled out the basket a little. The dragon had eaten all the bits of beefburger that he'd smuggled in from tea.

Alec produced the shed key. 'You've got a place of your own now, mate,' he said.

'Don't worry, though, I'll be there with you most of the time.' He made a face as he thought of what he'd let himself in for. 'I had to promise Grandad I'd get the allotment all ship-shape and Bristol fashion – that means tidy. You ought to see it! Well, you will. Should be lots of nice fresh insects for you, though.'

None of his books had been very helpful on the subject of baby dragon feeding. He knew that dragons were a sort of reptile, although some books called them worms. Alec thought that was a bit daft –

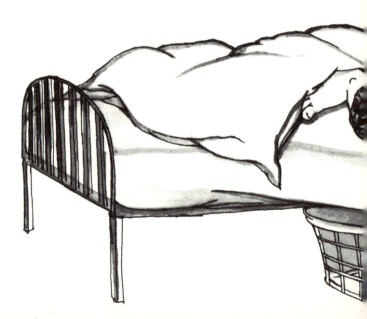

anyone could see they didn't look a bit like worms. He picked up one of his books and looked down the contents page. He read the story titles out (except for *Dragon Slayer*) but his pet didn't show any preference, just gazed up at him with unblinking yellow eyes.

'Aha, *Damian and the Dragon*, you'll like this one, mate. Hey – that's a good name. All right, Damian?' He settled back happily and read the story of Damian and the Dragon to Damian the Dragon.

Down at the Allotment
Chapter 2

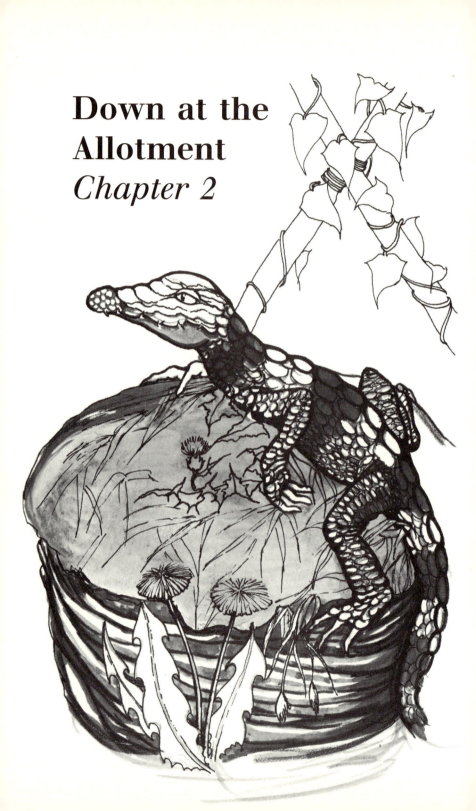

Alec woke up early that Sunday. It was another fine day, a real long hot summer, as his mum would say. He crept round the flat so as not to disturb her Sunday lie-in. In the kitchen he found a cardboard box with a lid on. It still smelled of soap powder but that couldn't be helped. He looked in the fridge. There was some shepherd's pie in there, left over from Friday's tea. He was supposed to have eaten it for his lunch yesterday but had forgotten all about it in the excitement. He scooped it out of the dish and dumped it into the box. Then he sneaked back to his room and added one baby dragon to the contents of the box. He closed the lid, threw the remains of his tee-shirts on to the top of his wardrobe, and smuggled the box out of the flat.

Alec had a nasty moment on the way to the allotment. At that time on a Sunday, there weren't many people about. It just so happened though, that their paper-boy was in Alec's class. They met in the backyard, where Wiggy (whose real name was Curtis Wilkinson) had left his bike and was

sorting through his big grey canvas bag.

'Hello, Alec. You're up early, What you got in the box, then?'

'Oh, hello, Wiggy. Nothing.'

'Here, d'you want your paper? Save me a journey – why's the box making that noise?'

'Oh, it's nothing – there's just some, er, things in there sliding around. See you then, Wiggy.'

'But it's scratching! Let's have a look – it's a gerbil, isn't it? Bet it's a gerbil.'

'No, honest – it's not a gerbil. Look, I've *got* to go, Wiggy, see you tomorrow.'

Alec sidled round the other boy and practically ran up the steps into the street.

Wiggy shook his head and turned back to his papers. 'The kid's puddled,' he said. 'Definitely daft.'

Meanwhile, Alec scuttled up the road, hoping he wouldn't meet anyone *else* he knew. The scrabbling sounds from the box sounded really loud in the still morning. He'd have liked to show Wiggy his new pet but Wiggy had lots of friends at school and the temptation to tell them about it would have been too much. Alec blushed at the thought of how they'd tease him. It was bad enough when he'd taken his *Dungeons and Dragons* game into school one day. Nearly everyone had laughed. They wouldn't laugh at a fully-grown dragon though, would they? He sighed. Maybe he *would* tell Wiggy – he wasn't too bad. It'd be nice to have a proper friend. Apart from Damian, of course.

Alec had a funny feeling that if anyone found out about Damian, he wouldn't be able to keep him. After all, little dragons didn't come crawling out of the loo every day, did they? And where had he come from in the first place? He didn't think

there'd been dragons in England for years.
Maybe it was the hot weather. He hugged
the box to himself fiercely. No one was
going to take Damian away. No one.

The allotments ran between the river
and some factories. There weren't many
cultivated ones now – the soil was poor
and people didn't seem to have time to

spend. Mostly they belonged to pensioners like Grandad who had time to make compost heaps and dig them in.

The allotment was deserted when Alec and Damian arrived. This meant Damian could get some fresh air and exercise. Alec hoped he wasn't allergic to it, too.

'Here we are, then, Damian. You can sunbathe while you watch me do all the work. We'll dig up some worms for you. Bet you're hungry.'

Damian hadn't eaten the shepherd's pie but Alec didn't really blame him. It hadn't looked very appetising spread out on the bottom of the box. Smelled of soap powder too. Alec tipped it out into the river.

Grandad's allotment was one of the ones right next door to the river. That gave him a bit of extra land because of the river-bank and the willow trees growing on it. It made the soil better too, especially in hot weather like this. Grandad's lettuce crop had gone berserk! Most of them had gone to seed; Grandad said they'd 'bolted'. They looked like pale brussels sprouts. Alec was supposed to put them all on the

compost heap because no one liked bolted
lettuce – they were too tough.

Damian seemed quite happy.
He wandered about for a while, his head
turning this way and that – as though he
was listening while Alec chattered to him:

'Don't wander off, mate – we'll have to
get you a little collar and a big long lead,
eh? We don't want you falling in the river!'

Alec watched in horror as his pet
suddenly darted forward with surprising
speed. His pink tongue rolled itself round
a frog and carried it to his mouth.

'Ugh, it was *alive*,' muttered Alec, and he
shut his eyes when the dragon made
several similar raids on the undergrowth.

Finally Damian climbed up on to the
dustbin bag that Alec was using to collect
all the stuff for the compost heap.
He settled down on some thistles and lay
there, still as a stone in the hot sunshine.

Alec's face grew redder than his hair.
His glasses slid down his sweaty nose and
he pulled up several carrots and spring
onions by mistake. 'Hell's bells, it's hot,'
he said.

He stood up, wiped his glasses on his
tee-shirt and his hands on his jeans,
and looked round. Over the jungle of
hogweed and collapsing runner-beans he
could see that the allotment was still pretty
quiet. There was a young family working
the strip at the far side, near the road.

They had neat rows of every kind of
vegetable you could think of, and some
you couldn't! The mother and father
looked exactly alike except the father had
a beard. The two children wore the same
kind of clothes as their parents. They had
odd names – something like Kennel and
Saffron as far as Alec could make out.
Grandad's hippies.

Alec smiled – *they* wouldn't come nosing
around, they were far too busy. Neither
would old Mr Bulstrode, who was the only
other person Alec could see. He was too
busy sitting outside his shed on a
deckchair, smoking his pipe and reading
the Sunday papers. Grandad said Mr

Bulstrode only came to get away from his wife, and to get some peace and quiet. Nobody bothered Mr Bulstrode and he didn't bother anyone else.

With everything so peaceful Alec decided to get Damian's new home ready. The shed was neat and tidy – no holes or cracks that Damian could get through. Good job there was no lav! Alec smiled to himself.
He made sure all the tools, plastic bags and boxes of bonemeal were out of the way. Then he made a bed of nice clean sacks in the cardboard box and put it in a corner.

'I'll have to save up and get you a collar and some chain – like a guard dog.' Alec chuckled at the idea. Imagine, Damian at Crufts. He started to laugh. 'Hey – Damian the wonder dog. Ha, ha! One man and his dragon.' He rolled about on the floor and Damian smiled his toothy smile.

Dragon in the River
Chapter 3

A lec spent the next four days nearly sick with impatience. He hated to leave his pet locked in the shed for so long, even though he spent every spare minute with him. He didn't like school much at the best of times. His marks were OK but his teachers always said he could do better if he would concentrate more and stop daydreaming. Daydreaming – huh! If only they knew. He saw Wiggy in class of course. Sometimes Wiggy would delay his games of football in the playground and come to say hello. Once he even asked Alec if he'd like to play. Alec was no good at football, though, or any other sport come to that. Still it was nice to be asked, even if all the other kids *did* groan and make daft remarks. Wiggy had forgotten all about last Sunday. He never asked about the box again.

After what seemed like a hundred years, end of term finally came. Six whole weeks of summer stretched ahead. Plenty of time for dragon training and for dragon-proofing the allotment.

On the first day of the holidays Alec's

mum told him that because he'd been so helpful lately she'd decided to give him extra pocket money (Thanks, Damian! he thought). Inspired by this he decided to get up an hour earlier and use the time to wash cars for fifty pence each. His mum was practically speechless, but not quite.

'A changed boy, he is,' she said to Mrs Biggs one day. 'He never lies in bed all morning, always out and about. And Grandad's allotment is coming on a treat.'

'I expect it's all this nice weather,' said Mrs Biggs. 'I always says it's a sin to lie in bed when the sun's shining.'

Alec was saving up. He reckoned that he should soon have enough money to get three metres of plastic chain – the sort you can use to padlock your bike to things. He was going to make sure Damian didn't give him another fright. It had happened like this:

On the fourth day of the holidays he and Damian had both been sunbathing. Alec wasn't used to all the hard work he'd been doing and had fallen asleep. He woke up suddenly with a feeling that something

was wrong. He sat up and looked around.
Damian had been lying in the
wheelbarrow – now he was gone. Alec
scrambled to his feet in panic.

'Damian!' he yelled. 'Here, Damian!
Where are you?'

He'd forgotten all about being secretive.
Luckily only old Mr Bulstrode was nearby,
and he was asleep under his newspaper.
With a sinking heart Alec stumbled

towards the river. It was here, of course, where most of the frogs could be found.

'Damian,' his voice was a hoarse whisper. 'Oh no! Damian.'

Alec hadn't been able to see him at first, then suddenly there he was, floating in the water, looking for all the world like a drifting log.

'He's drowned,' wailed Alec. He grabbed a willow branch, and, kneeling on the bank, he reached out as far as he could. Damian floated out of reach, amongst some water-lilies. At the same moment that Alec lost his balance he saw that Damian's legs were not just hanging down uselessly, they were lazily paddling. With a great splash, Alec entered the water. He came up, spluttering and coughing, by Damian's side. Damian gave a flick of his tail and shot away from him. Alec's feet sank into the clinging mud as he thrashed about.

'Oh no,' he spluttered, '*I'm* drowning
now. Come *here*, Damian.' He freed one
foot from the mud and staggered forward.
Another flick and Damian was swimming
easily, always just out of reach.

Alec sat down heavily in the mud.
The river was only about half a metre
deep there. Alec knew that it was much
deeper in the middle, though, and there
was quite a strong current. He stayed
where he was. He could feel the smelly
mud seeping into his underpants. Damian,
quite at home, stayed where he was, too.
His head was just above the water.

He stared at Alec through half-closed eyes.

Alec was very close to tears. He was about to give in to them when Damian flicked his tail again. The next moment he was climbing on to the bank. He took a few steps and then lay there, glistening. He seemed to be waiting for Alec. He looked at him as if to say, 'Come on, are you going to stay in there all day?'

With great difficulty and a horrid sucking noise, Alec stood up. He moved forward and fell face down into the water. Very slowly, on hands and knees, he crawled out. Out of habit, the first thing he did was to check his glasses. They were still there. Behind them was the only bit of Alec that wasn't covered in greenish-brown slime. He looked down at himself. His tee-shirt hung around his knees, his trainers were oozing with the stuff. The smell was so awful that he had to breathe through his mouth. Damian waddled towards the shed and Alec followed him squelchily.

'Didn't know dragons could swim, did I?' he muttered.

When his mum found out that Alec had fallen into the river (there was no way he could keep *that* from her), Alec had to use every trick he knew to stop her from putting the allotment out of bounds.
He finally calmed her down by agreeing to have his name put down for Saturday morning swimming lessons at the baths.

As soon as he could, Alec went to buy that chain and a small dog-collar.
He found that he had enough money left to get something for his mum, so he bought the biggest bunch of freesias that he could afford. When he gave them to her she said, 'Your dad used to give me these,' then she started to cry quietly and hurried into the kitchen so he wouldn't see. Not for the first time, Alec thought how peculiar grown-ups were.

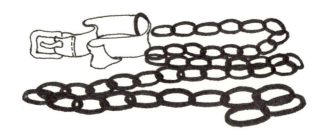

Drought
Chapter 4

That summer was the best anyone could remember. People stayed out of doors till late in the evening. The small area of grass that belonged to Alec's flats was always full of people lounging in deckchairs or just sitting on the ground. Old ladies sat, knees apart, holding their handbags and fanning themselves with white hankies. They said that summers were always like this when they were girls.

Eventually the grass turned brown and dusty. The Government declared a drought and they appointed a Minister for the drought. He went on television and said that everyone must save water. People weren't allowed to wash their cars unless they used old bathwater. Alec's car-wash business became quiet. Grandad was worried about his allotment again. Alec offered to dig irrigation ditches from the river, but his mum said he wasn't to go near it again. Not till he'd got his green badge, anyway.

By the end of the third week of the holidays they'd still had no rain and Alec was worried. The frogs, which had always been so plentiful around the allotment, had disappeared. Alec wasn't sure if that was because of the drought or Damian. In any case, something must be done about feeding him. Alec tried all sorts of things, until finally he found that if he left a dish of cat food in the corner of the shed for a few days Damian would eventually eat it.

Pretty disgusting, he thought, but then Damian might feel the same way about salad-cream sandwiches.

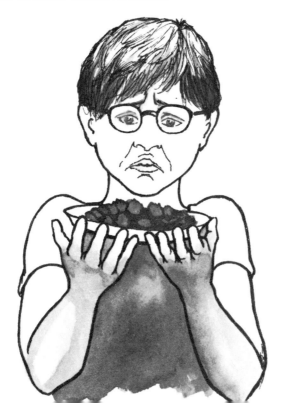

The hot weather and the aging cat food were making the shed rather smelly, so Alec took to reading Damian's bedtime story outside. He was doing this one night, leaning comfortably against the wheelbarrow, when a voice said, 'What kind of animal is *that?*'

Alec dropped the book and leaped to his feet. One of the hippy children stood there, staring open-mouthed.

'What is it?' it repeated, pointing at Damian who lay there taking the evening sun.

'Oh, it's ah, it's a plastic dinosaur –
it's not *real* !'

'Why does it have on a collar and lead
then?'

'That's just for show – it's a scarecrow,
you see.' Alec kept his fingers crossed
behind his back, hoping against hope that
Damian would keep up his frozen-log
impression.

The child stared at Damian for what
seemed like ages but, luckily, Damian
didn't move.

Alec tried to think of something to
distract the awful kid. 'Does your dad
know you're here?' he finally said.

'Oh, yes,' said the child firmly. 'Gavin says we have nothing to fear from our environment.'

Alec stared, open mouthed. He was more impressed by 'Gavin' than he was by enviry-whatsit. He tried an old trick.

'Listen, I can hear your dad shouting for you,' he said.

'He's not there, actually,' said the grotty tot. 'We just came with Theodora today.'

Alec winced. 'Isn't Theodora afraid you'll fall in the river?' he asked without much hope. He wondered if he dared push the kid in, but decided against it. A bright idea came to him. 'You know there's lots of *leeches* around here, don't you? They're kind of water-slugs that stick on to you and suck your blood. *I've* got some special cream to keep them off,' he added hastily, 'only it's at home.' He began to stare fixedly at the child's bare legs and feet. 'You can't pull them off you know, they burrow under your skin and suck all the blood. Then they lay eggs in you and . . . '

It was enough. With a howl of disgust the child disappeared through the

undergrowth, wailing for Theodora.

This left Alec with yet another problem. Security. He had made sure about keeping Damian in; what about keeping unwanted visitors *out*? After a bit of thought he came up with a pretty good solution.

Using the runner-bean frame, the shed, and a willow tree as corner posts, he stretched long lengths of strong black cotton around the plot. It was called buttonhole thread and he had to buy three reels of it. He tied it at about waist height to an adult (neck height to a little kid,

he thought with a nasty smirk). It was very nearly invisible, especially if you weren't looking for it. Before he tied it, though, he threaded it through some plastic beakers. Just a few, in twos, well spaced out. When he tried walking into the thread the beakers rattled together and made just enough noise to act as a warning.
If anyone asked he'd tell them it was a bird scarer.

For a while things were nice and quiet. The hot summer wore on. Alec even managed to harvest some beans and carrots. He thought he'd manage some decent potatoes too, later on. Grandad said he'd done wonders, what with the dry weather and all.

Damian had soon got used to his collar and chain – it didn't even bother him when he wore it in the river. Alec held on to one end while Damian swam about happily amongst the water-lilies.

Alec concentrated hard on teaching his dragon how to be more dragonish. None of his books featured water-loving dragons; indeed, Alec often worried in case Damian's fondness for the river should somehow interfere with the growth of his real dragon features. The wings weren't so much of a problem. Alec was convinced that he could see them growing like little buds amongst the scales that were developing quite quickly on his pet's back. It was the fire-breathing bit that worried him, of course. Everyone knows that fire and water don't mix. Damian was bombarded with stories and pictures of the days of old when knights were bold and dragons were, well, dragons.

Alec took some comfort from Damian's reactions to cats, though. Just recently, he'd found several hanging around – attracted by the smell of Damian's mouldy snacks, Alec supposed. He'd been quite anxious when he'd first started shooing them away from the shed one morning. One huge one-eared tabby looked quite capable of attacking a poor baby dragon.

'Gerroudofit, moggie,' Alec growled, clapping his hands as he ran towards it. The cat stepped back a few paces, its tail in the air. 'Go on, shoo, shoo.' It sat down, stretched one leg out before it, and began to lick its toes. 'Hmm, pity you can't frazzle it yet, mate,' he said, as he bustled around tidying up the shed and clipping on Damian's chain. 'Shame you can't send it off with its tail singed.'

Alec emerged from the shed with the wheelbarrow, giving the cat a dirty look. Damian waddled behind him. When the cat saw Damian it froze, all its fur standing on end. Damian froze too, then he charged. To Alec's astonishment (and the cat's) he was almost upon it before the cat recovered enough to disappear, spitting and yowling, up into the nearest willow tree. Damian, at the end of his chain, opened his mouth and hissed back.

'Wow!' said Alec, expecting at any
minute to see the willow burst into flames.
'You little *tiger*. That's shown *him*,' he said.
Damian grinned up at him and Alec
scratched his head thoughtfully. Then he
picked him up and put him in the
wheelbarrow. 'We'll have an early story
today, Damian. I think *The Terrible-
Tempered Dragon* might be nice, don't
you?' He settled down on a small patch of
grass and began to read. Each time he
turned the page on to a new picture,
he held the book up so Damian could see.

The cat stayed up in the tree till well
after dark.

Problems
Chapter 5

'Alec, dear,' said his mum a week later. 'Would you mind popping in to see Mrs Biggs on your way to the supermarket? Just to see if she needs anything.'

'OK, Mum.' It was breakfast time and Alec was busy with his Coco Pops.

'Here's my list and the money.' She put a large brown purse on the kitchen table. 'Don't get the change muddled up and don't forget to put the frozen things into the freezer.'

'OK, Mum.'

'I've got to dash, I'll be late for work – oh, and Alec . . . '

'Yes, Mum?'

'Keep a look out for Mrs Biggs's Jonty, will you – he's gone missing and you know how much she thinks of her cat.'

'OK, Mum.'

Alec's mum left for work and Alec, in a hurry to get back to Damian, picked up the purse and went to find Mrs Biggs.

'Are you in a rush as usual, young man? I don't know, you've gone from one extreme to the other, why it only seems like yesterday . . .'

Alec sighed and hoped this wouldn't go on too long. He tried to distract her. 'Sorry, Mrs B., I *am* in a bit of a rush. I'll have a bit of a look round for Jonty while I'm out – Mum said he was missing again.'

Mrs Biggs's face fell. 'Oh, if only you would, love – I know I'm silly really but he *has* had the operation – he shouldn't wander. Not like Mrs Evans' Ginger. *He's* been gone for three days, you know. I *told* her to get him seen to.'

Alec began to feel uneasy. Mrs Biggs went on and on.

'Course, they go a bit greedy and sleepy after the operation, but at least they don't

wander.' Her face clouded. 'At least, they're not *supposed* to – mind, that big black thing from across the yard – him with the bell on his collar – well *he* went last week and I know for a fact ...'

Alec wasn't listening any more. His imagination was conjuring up horrible pictures. He shook his head to send them away.

'... and so I said to her, I said, they just bundle them off into the back of a van and goodness knows where they end up. Fur coats, I shouldn't wonder. Here, Alec, come back – you haven't got my *list*.'

Alec made it to the allotment in record time. He flung the shed door open. Damian gazed at him from his bed.

'Damian, you haven't, have you?' He searched around, looking for grisly remains. He'd half-expected to see ears and a tail sticking out of Damian's mouth.

He clipped on the chain and went outside. He looked in the long grass all round the shed. Then he searched amongst the weeds and wildflowers that he'd left as a screen. Nothing. Everything

looked as normal as a dragon's garden
could look.

'Sorry, mate,' said Alec. 'I just got in a
panic, Come on, how about a swim? Think
I could do with one as well.' He flung off
his clothes and, with one end of the chain
round his wrist, leaped in as far from
the bank as he could, to avoid the mud.
He showed Damian the results of the
swimming club. He could now manage a
fairly presentable breast-stroke. Damian
demonstrated some stylish flicks. They
floated around for ages. The river was low
and sluggish with the lack of rain. It was
still cool and wet though, and that was all
that mattered, really.

Alec couldn't avoid the mud when they finally clambered out. He rinsed his toes at the standpipe and the friends lay down in their usual places and let the warm sun dry them.

'The weatherman said we'll have some rain soon,' said Alec, squinting up at the sky. 'Hope we do, maybe it will bring the frogs back.' Damian's tongue flicked and caught an unwary beetle. 'Hmm, I don't think you'll go hungry, mate.'

Alec sat up to look at his pet and then he noticed the big brown purse lying on the ground beside the shed door. 'Uh, oh, I'm in a spot of bother, mate. Oh, no, I'm *dead*! It's early-closing day.'

He grabbed his watch from the top of the pile of clothes. 'Great! I've still got half an hour.' He pulled on his clothes, then stood looking uncertainly at Damian. He looked round the allotment. No one about. He made sure the chain was properly fastened, then grabbed the purse.

'Be right back, Damian, you stay there.'
He dashed off. It did seem a shame to lock
poor old Damian in that shed in the
middle of a good sunbathe.

After a mad dash round the
supermarket, made worse because his
trolley had a seized-up front wheel, Alec
dumped the shopping into the kitchen.
Then he crept past Mrs Biggs's flat (he'd
remembered too late about *her* shopping).

He was back at the allotment in no time.
Damian was gone! The chain lay in the
grass, one end still fastened to the shed.
Alec picked up the end that should have
been fastened to Damian. It had been
undone.

A thought struck him. He wheeled
round. There was Theodora bending over
her vegetables with a dutch hoe. Halfway
between Alec and Theodora was a little
figure toddling along with out-stretched
arms. In the outstretched arms lay
Damian. Alec had never moved so fast!
With a wonderful flying tackle he had the
child lying flat on its face. Ignoring the
screeching kid, Alec gathered up Damian,

and ran back to the shed. He'd just locked
the door and was leaning against it,
puffing and panting, when the rattle of the
bird scarer and some very unlady-like
language told him he was no longer alone.
He turned to face Theodora. She was
trying to free herself from the bird scarer.
Her face was very red.

'You little monster – how *dare* you!'
She demolished the bird scarer and
advanced towards him. Alec cringed.
All that gardening was bound to have
developed her muscles. 'Fancy knocking

down poor little Saffron – you rotten bully! Lucky for you I'm into non-violence.' She made up for it with her tongue, though.

With his face almost as red as Theodora's, Alec listened to some really horrible abuse. Finally she swept away saying, 'I know who you are – I'm going straight round to see your mum.'

Alec crept into the shed and lay beside Damian. 'I wish you were older and your wings had grown,' he said. 'Then we could just fly away.'

When Alec got home his mum was waiting in the kitchen. She stood with her arms folded, two plastic carriers at her feet. Their contents had melted and formed puddles on the lino.

'Alec, what is the matter with you?' she said quietly. 'I've only just got in from work, Alec, I'm tired.' He opened his mouth to speak, then thought better of it. 'That hippy woman was waiting for me in the backyard, Alec, then I saw Mrs Biggs. Then I got in here and saw this.'

She pointed with her foot at the soggy
shopping. 'Just go to your room, will you.
You can stay in tomorrow too, there's
plenty to be done around here.'

Alec found his voice. 'But Mum, I can't!
I . . . ' The look on her face told him not to
argue any more.

Alec had a bad night. He woke next
morning in a cold sweat after a nightmare
in which his mother had ordered him to
put his armour on and go and kill the
terrible dragon that was threatening the
lovely Princess Theodora. It was another
lovely day, which made him feel worse,
somehow.

It was early. Maybe if he was mega-quiet
he could slip down for a quick visit and be

back before his mum woke up. He was just tip-toeing past her bedroom when she called out, 'Alec, take a pound out of my purse and see if you can catch Curtis – I forgot to pay for the papers yesterday, what with one thing and another.'

With a deep sigh Alec went in search of Wiggy. He found him on the floor below, trying to push a thick bundle of papers through a letterbox.

'More haste less speed, eh, Alec?' Wiggy grinned and began to post the papers one at a time. 'You off down the allotments?'

'Not today, Wiggy, I've been grounded.'

Wiggy looked impressed. 'How long for?' he asked.

'Just today, I think. She'll probably have calmed down by tomorrow, specially if I'm a real creep and do some jobs for her.'

Wiggy nodded. 'Do the washing-up without being asked,' he advised. 'That always gets 'em. Anyway, one day isn't too bad.'

Alec took a deep breath. 'Well, as a matter of fact it is. For Damian, anyway.'

'Who?'

'Damian. He's my pet. I keep him in the shed down there.'

'Oh, hey! *That's* what was in the box. Damian. What is it, anyway?'

'A baby dragon.'

Wiggy burst into loud laughter. 'OK, Alec, *don't* tell me then.'

Alec got rather agitated. 'It is, it *is*! Honest, Wiggy – it's a dragon – a *baby* dragon. It crawled up the lav one morning.' He blurted out the whole story. 'Look, *you* could go down there. I'll give you the key. Here. Just fasten the end of the chain on to his collar. He likes to swim a bit, then sunbathe.' Alec was gabbling. He had to get back to the flat before his mum got suspicious. 'Only please, *please* don't tell anyone.'

'Huh, I wouldn't *dare*,' said Wiggy.

'They'd think I was as daft as you.'

He chose the next bundle of papers.

'I'll have a ride over this afternoon.
I should be OK. He won't mistake me for
St George, I'm the wrong colour.'

Laughing at his own joke he disappeared
down the corridor, leaving Alec to climb
the stairs slowly and wonder if he'd done
the right thing.

Alec had just finished scrubbing the last
saucepan when he saw Wiggy riding into
the yard. Oh no, he thought angrily,
he's *never* had time to see to Damian
properly. He turned away from the window
and was wiping the work surface when
the doorbell rang.

He heard his mum come out of the
living-room where she was watching an
old film on television. 'Hello, Curtis,
not still delivering the papers surely?'

'Hello, Mrs Sinclair. Erm – can Alec
come out to play?'

Alec could hear the surprise in his
mother's voice. 'Oh, well, I'm afraid he has
to stay in today, Curtis. You can come in
and see him for a minute, though.'

She didn't want to turn Wiggy away
because she couldn't remember the last
time anyone had come round to play with
Alec.

'Alec. Here's Curtis to see you.'
She lowered her voice. 'He's been rather
naughty, so he's being punished today.
He can come out tomorrow, though,'
she finished anxiously.

'Oh, that's good because I was
wondering if he'd like to come to the zoo
with me tomorrow.'

A strange feeling came over Alec when
he heard this. He went out into the hall.
'Hello, Wiggy,' he said. Wiggy was staring
at him, a fixed smile on his face.

'H – hello, Alec. Would you like to come
to the zoo tomorrow? It's only a pound.'
Wiggy stole a quick glance at Alec's mum

to make sure she wasn't looking at him.
Then he started nodding frantically at
Alec. His eyes were like saucers.

'Oh, is it OK, Mum?'

'Well, yes, all right then, but I don't know
why you're looking so miserable about it.'
She went back into the living-room.

'You can stay a little while, Curtis. Don't
forget he's still in disgrace, though.'

'Come and see my *Dungeons and* . . .
er . . . come and see my games, Wiggy.'
Alec grabbed the other boy and hustled
him into his bedroom. He closed the door.
'What's all this zoo rubbish – what about
Damian?'

'You great stupid *gommo*,' Wiggy hissed
back. 'You know what you've got there?
That's no baby dragon, mate – that's a
bloomin' baby *crocodile!*'

All the anger went out of Alec and he
sat down heavily on his bed. Wiggy sat
down beside him and put his arm around
Alec's shoulders. To his horror Alec felt
the tears begin to well up inside him.

Wiggy was trying his best to comfort
him. 'You *can't* keep him. You must see
that. For one thing, what'll happen in the
winter? crocodiles need hot weather, don't
they? He might *die*!'

Alec wasn't comforted. 'He's *mine*,'
he whispered.

'OK, then,' said Wiggy. 'S'pose you *did*
keep him and he didn't freeze to death.
He'd probably eat you when he got bigger.
You'd look after him and feed him and
that, then he'd pay you back by *eating* you.
Anyway, there's probably a law against

keeping alligators and crocodiles.'

He became a bit impatient. 'You must've known he wasn't a dragon – there's no such *thing*.'

Alec leaped to his feet, his eyes blazing. 'There damned well *is*,' he yelled. Then he clapped his hand over his mouth.

'Alec!' his mother's voice floated in from the front room.

'Look, I'm sorry, Alec.' Wiggy stood up to leave. 'We've just *got* to take him to the zoo. Or would you rather I just went and told your mum?'

Alec was defeated. 'Sorry I shouted at you,' he mumbled.

'That's OK, mate, I know how you feel. See you tomorrow, then.' He left Alec alone.

'Oh no, you don't know how I feel. You don't know at all,' Alec said to himself. He was still staring into space an hour later when his mum put her head round the door.

'Cheer up, dear,' she said. 'It was nice of Curtis to think of you. You'll have a lovely day at the zoo.'

Damian's New Home
Chapter 6

Wiggy stood waiting at the bus-stop next morning. He wasn't feeling much better than Alec. He watched the awkward red-haired boy shuffling towards him, the sunlight glinting off his glasses. Alec had a sack clutched in his arms – no need to ask what was in *there*, Wiggy thought. He remembered how shocked he'd been the day before. He'd opened the shed door expecting to see a lizard or a newt. When he'd seen Damian gazing steadily back at him he'd had the surprise of his life.

He tried to look cheerful. 'Come on, mate. It won't be all that bad, you'll see.'

Alec didn't answer. He didn't speak at all until the bus started off. Then the sack on his knees began to bulge and bounce. He nudged Wiggy. 'How far is it? He doesn't like being in a sack.'

'Well, let him out then.'

'But everyone will *see*.'

'It doesn't really matter *now*, does it?'

Alec opened up the sack and Damian immediately stuck his head out. Then he climbed up Alec and put his head over his shoulder. He seemed quite happy there, gazing at the woman sitting behind them. A sudden sharp gasp told them that the woman had noticed Damian and wasn't quite so happy. Alec turned and smiled sweetly at her. She just carried on staring at Damian.

Alec turned back to Wiggy. 'He does take you by surprise when you first see him, doesn't he?'

Wiggy nodded. 'You don't see many crocodiles in the West Midlands.'

Alec seemed to be cheering up, so Wiggy chatted on. 'Bet he's grown a bit – don't think he'd be able to get down the lav any more. How big do crocodiles get, anyway?'

'Don't know anything about crocodiles, Wiggy.'

Just then Damian moved a few centimetres up Alec's chest. The lady behind them hurriedly gathered up her things and rang the bell. Alec could see her standing at the bus-stop, still gazing after the bus till it turned a corner and was out of sight.

'I don't think that was really her stop,' Wiggy whispered in his ear. For some reason this sent them off into fits of laughter.

They'd just about got themselves under control when the man in front turned round and said, ''Scuse me, sonny – what have you been feeding your lizard on?'

'It's not a lizard,' giggled Alec, 'it's a crocodile.'

'Oh, that's it then,' said the man and turned back to his newspaper.

Alec was almost cheerful as they got off the bus and headed for the zoo gates.

The man in the ticket office picked up a telephone. 'Now then, Arthur,' he said into it, 'you'd best come to the main gate – there's something you ought to see.'

He came out of the ticket office and put a hand on Wiggy's shoulder. 'Hang on a bit, lad,' he said. 'We don't want your mate there getting into trouble, do we?'

He smiled at Alec but stayed as far away from him as he could. 'If I'm not mistaken, sonny, what you've got there is a young crocodile. Now what are you doing with one of those on your shoulder, eh?'

At that moment they were joined by a young man wearing a white coat and a broad grin. He leaned forward and studied Damian. 'Well I'll be blowed!' he said. 'What a magnificent specimen! Nile crocodile if I'm not mistaken. About eighteen months to two years I'd say. Oh, I'm sorry, young man, I'm Arthur Fellows, I run the reptile house.' He shook hands with Alec.

'I'm Alec, this is Curtis, and this is

Damian,' Alec said rather proudly. He was
enjoying all the attention.

Arthur shook hands with Wiggy and
scratched Damian's head. 'Look, we seem
to be attracting a bit of a crowd here –
let's go to my office.'

DAMIAN : NILOTIC CROCODILE
(CROCODYLUS NILOTICUS)
RANGE : AFRICA AND MADAGASCAR.
LENGTH IN FEET : 12 – 16
PRESENTED BY ALISTAIR SINCLAIR,
AGED 11, OF WOLVERHAMPTON.

Alec, Wiggy and Arthur stood in front of Damian's new home. Alec and Wiggy both wore flat black hats with 'Keeper' embroidered in red above the peak. Arthur had made them honorary keepers. This meant a permanent free pass into the zoo for both of them.

Arthur had been delighted with Alec's story of how he and Damian first met. He wasn't so happy with whoever had first got hold of Damian, though. 'You hear about this kind of thing happening in America,' he said. 'People get them as private pets when they're a few weeks old – they're only tiny then, about twenty centimetres long. People don't realise how quickly they grow. Poor old Damian must have been in the sewers for a while. Luckily for him – and for us – he found you, Alec. You've done a grand job caring for him. I can see I'll have to watch out for *my* job in a few years time. Till then I hope we'll see you in here every Saturday – there's plenty for you to do and you can keep an eye on Damian, make sure we're looking after him properly.'

Later that afternoon Wiggy and Alec were in the Ape House, making faces at the orang-utans, when they heard their names being called over the loudspeaker. They hurried importantly back to the Reptile House. Arthur was waiting with a newspaper reporter and a photographer. Alec told his story (he didn't mention dragons at all). Then Damian was taken from his case, to pose with Alec and Wiggy. Alec knew that this was probably the last time he'd ever hold him, so his smile for the camera was a bit wobbly. Arthur said he would take the two boys home and have a chat with Alec's mum, before she saw the paper!

Alec's mum came out of the kitchen
when she heard voices in the hall.
She was still wearing her overall from
work and she had a potato peeler in one
hand. She put that in her pocket and
shook hands with Arthur but when he said
who he was her face fell.

'Oh no, what have they done?' she said.

'See. I *told* you she'd say that!' said Alec,
crossly.

Arthur and Wiggy both laughed,
his mum just looked puzzled. 'I think
you'd better come and sit down while I
explain, Mrs Sinclair – don't look so
worried.'

Alec and Wiggy had just begun a game of snap when they heard a loud shriek from the kitchen.

'He's just told her the bit about the loo,' Alec grinned at his friend. 'Hey, what if she'd been sitting on it at the time!'

'Tell you what,' giggled Wiggy, 'if *my* mum had been sitting on it, Damian would have been suffocated to death!'

The two boys amused themselves with thoughts like this until they heard Arthur come out of the kitchen. Alec's mum was behind him, her face flushed.

'Alec, you naughty boy – why didn't you *tell* me? No wonder you suddenly got green fingers.' She was trying to sound cross but not quite succeeding. 'Well, thank goodness Curtis has some sense,' she said. 'Now you *will* stay for tea, won't you, Curtis? By the way,' she added, 'Mrs Biggs found Jonty – he'd been adopted by Katy Jarvis from flat twelve!'